A TALE FROM
THE BROTHERS GRIMM

KING GRISLY-BEARD

You can read this book as you listen to the cassette tape which accompanies it.
Turn the pages when you hear the tone signals.

Editor: Alma Gilleo   Story Adaptation: James R. Robertson   Illustrations: Krystyna Stasiak   Book Design: Robert Borja

SVE
SOCIETY FOR VISUAL EDUCATION, INC.

1345 Diversey Parkway, Chicago, Illinois 60614
A Business Corporation

ISBN 0-89290-004-0 Dewey Decimal Number 398.2

Printed in U.S.A.

Once upon a time there lived a very beautiful princess named Alice. Alice's father was a wise old king, and he was very proud of his daughter because she was so beautiful.

Alice's hair was long and silky, and her eyes sparkled like diamonds. But most of the time her eyes were full of spite, for Alice liked nothing more than making fun of other people.

Alice even made fun of a noble young king from a neighboring land, who wanted to marry her. "Why you look like a grisly old mop! I'm going to call you King Grisly-Beard from now on!" Alice told him.

Alice's father heard this remark, and it made him very angry. So he decided on a plan to make Alice more humble.

"You're too high and mighty for your own good, Alice," her father said. "I'm going to make you marry the next beggar that comes to this castle."

And sure enough, the very next day, a poor, traveling musician arrived at the castle. He sang:

"Robins gathered in the treetops
Sing a song of light and spring,
As evening falls in dewy drops
On every feathered wing."

"Come into the castle, musician, come inside. I want you to marry my daughter — if you'll have her," the king said.

When Alice heard this news, she begged, cried, screamed and kicked, for she did not want to marry a poor musician. But her father had decided to teach her a lesson, and he would not change his mind.

So angry Alice and the poor musician were married that very day. And as soon as the wedding was over, the newlyweds left the castle and started walking to the musician's tiny faraway cottage.

Soon they reached the edge of an enormous rolling meadow.

"Why this meadow stretches on as far as I can see! Who does it belong to?" Alice asked.

"It belongs to the man who wanted to marry you — the king you made fun of and called a grisly old mop," her husband told her.

And when they walked on for many miles more, Alice saw a vast city in the distance.

"And whose city is that?" she asked.

"That, too, belongs to King Grisly-Beard. He is master and ruler of this whole kingdom."

"Oh, how foolish I was." Alice said. "I could have married King Grisly-Beard and all this would be mine."

Sad Alice and her new husband continued on their way, through a forest of dark trees. Finally they arrived at the tiny cottage that would be their home.

Alice rushed inside the cottage to look for the servants, but of course the poor musician had no servants. Princess Alice would have to do all the housework herself!

But Alice didn't know how to do even the simplest task, like lighting a cooking fire. Poor Alice had all kinds of problems.

Within a few days, for instance, the cupboard in the little cottage was completely bare. And this made Alice's husband very angry.

"Listen to me, wife," said her husband. "We can't go on like this. You'll have to learn a trade and earn some money, or soon we'll starve to death!"

So Alice tried to learn to spin and make cloth, but the sharp threads cut into her tender fingers. Alice wrapped tight bandages around her sore hands, and soon she couldn't even move her fingers at all!

"You're a good-for-nothing, Alice. You can't do any work," her husband said. "I'll give you another chance, though. I'll set up a trade for you in pots and pans, and maybe you can make some money that way."

So Alice set up a shop, in a little stall in the marketplace of a nearby town. She offered all kinds of pots and pans for sale.

Because Alice was so charming, many people flocked to her stall and she made a lot of money.

But suddenly one day a soldier on a wild horse came galloping through the market and plowed right through Alice's stall. The soldier and his horse destroyed all the pots and pans, and put poor frightened Alice right out of business.

But the musician had still another plan for his wife.

"Alice, I've been to the king's palace and they've agreed to hire you as a kitchen-maid. So be on your way!"

That very day Alice began working as a humble servant in the palace kitchen.

She had to do the dirtiest chores of all, like scrubbing floors and scraping out food from the huge black cooking kettles, then polishing the kettles until they sparkled.

But Alice was allowed to take leftovers and scraps of food home to her husband. At least the newlyweds wouldn't have to go hungry now.

One day, not long after Alice began working as a kitchen-maid, a royal parade passed by the kitchen door. Excitement was in the air, for today the young king would choose his bride.

As Alice looked at the parade, she began to weep softly to herself. "Oh, why was I so foolish and cruel? Why did I always make fun of everyone? Surely I deserve this punishment. I deserve to be a lowly servant in the kitchen."

There was going to be a great feast at the king's wedding.

So Alice packed a big basket full of food to take home. Just as she was leaving the kitchen, the king himself stepped into the doorway. And it was none other than King Grisly-Beard!

Alice trembled with fear. She turned to run away from the king, but tripped over her own feet and spilled the big basket. Alice was so embarrassed she wanted to sink into the floor and disappear.

But King Grisly-Beard was not angry. He stepped forth to comfort poor Alice. As he ripped off his grisly false beard, the king spoke to Alice.

"Fear not, kitchen-maid. Fear me not, for I was the poor musician who married you and made you spin until your fingers ached. And I was also the soldier who destroyed your pots and pans," he said.

"I did these things because I love you," the king said. "I wanted to make you humble and punish you for making fun of me. Now it is done. You've learned what it means to be humble, and you deserve to be my queen."

So humble, happy Alice and the young king celebrated their "true" marriage. They ruled their vast lands together for many years, and never again did Alice make fun of other people.

THE
SIX-BUTTON
DRAGON

THE
SIX-BUTTON
DRAGON

by

MATT ROBINSON

Illustrated by Brumsic Brandon, Jr.

RANDOM HOUSE

Once upon a long time ago, in the middle of the
Double-Dry Desert, there stood a mountain so high that
the clouds had to walk up a ladder just to get over it.
And they called this mountain "Mighty Mountain."

Now the way the story goes, no one was allowed to get near Mighty Mountain, because right beside the mountain, in a red-on-red striped tent with wall-to-wall sand that was hot as an oven cooking turkey, lived Fire-Breathing Brown, the Six-Button Dragon.

He had great red eyes, and fire shot out of his mouth like lightning bolts, and all around his scaly skin he wore a sharp six-button blazer. That's why they called him "the Six-Button Dragon."

Now, believe me, Fire-Breathing Brown, the Six-Button Dragon, would not let anybody near Mighty Mountain, because as far as he knew, that was his mountain.

Now one bright sunny day, Little Louella, the loveliest little lady you ever did see, was crossing the Double-Dry Desert to take a pail of stringbeans to her Cousin Clarice, who lived on the other side of the desert.

Well, it was so hot on the desert that when Little Louella
came to Mighty Mountain, she sat down in the shade
of the mountain, just to rest up and get herself together.

But no sooner did she sit down than Fire-Breathing
Brown, the Six-Button Dragon, looked up and saw her...

...and roared out of his tent, and smoke came out of
his nose and fire came out of his mouth...

...and he charged right toward
Little Louella.

Poor Little Louella was so scared that she dropped her pail of stringbeans and ran half-way up the mountain. But when she got to the middle of the mountain, that was as far as she could go.

Now Fire-Breathing Brown, the Six-Button Dragon, couldn't climb up the mountain, so he stayed down at the bottom and breathed those long streams of fire up at Little Louella. And the fire was getting closer and closer to that poor little girl.

Just then, who should appear at the top of the mountain but one of the toughest little guys in the whole wide world. And his name was Short-Stick Stokes. That's what everybody called him, Short-Stick Stokes.

He carried a short stick with him at all times, but he never used it unless a little girl was in trouble.

And when he saw Fire-Breathing Brown breathing fire
at Little Louella, Short-Stick Stokes whipped out his
short stick and started swinging DOWN at the
Six-Button Dragon.

And when the Six-Button Dragon looked up and saw Short-Stick Stokes swinging his short stick down, he started breathing his fire UP at him.

Well, the problem was that Fire-Breathing Brown, the Six-Button Dragon, was too far DOWN to reach Short-Stick Stokes, and Short-Stick Stokes was too far UP for his short stick to reach the Six-Button Dragon. In the meantime, poor Little Louella was in the MIDDLE, and she didn't care who was UP or who was DOWN, as long as she didn't get burned by the fire or hit by the stick.

Then, all of a sudden, Short-Stick Stokes had an idea.
He climbed down the other side of Mighty Mountain,
and ran *around* the mountain...

...until he came up *behind* the Six-Button Dragon.

He tied the pail of stringbeans onto the dragon's tail.
Then he took his short stick and whacked on that tail
so hard...

…that Fire-Breathing Brown, the Six-Button Dragon, jumped up and ran clean across the Double-Dry Desert with the stringbeans for Cousin Clarice.

Then Short-Stick Stokes climbed up to the middle of the mountain, rescued Little Louella, and took her up to the top of the mountain.

There they settled down, made a little garden
and raised stringbeans forever.